A Giant First-Start Reader

This easy reader contains only 48 different words, repeated often to help the young reader develop word recognition and interest in reading.

Basic word list for *The Jolly Monsters*

a	laughed	she
always	like	still
and	liked	story
at	listen	the
but	listened	there
face	look	this
friend	looked	time
funny	made	to
had	make	too
happy	monster	upon
he	name	very
her	never	Wally
his	not	was
Holly	once	what
jolly	picture	will
laugh	said	you

Once upon a time…

there was a monster.

Holly was her name.

Holly was a jolly monster.

She was always happy.

She liked to laugh.

Holly the jolly monster had a friend.

Wally was his name.

But Wally was not jolly like Holly.

Wally was never happy.

He never laughed.

"Look at this," said Holly.

"Look at the funny picture."

The funny picture made Holly laugh.

Wally looked—but he never laughed.

"Listen," said Holly.

"Listen to this funny story."

The funny story made Holly laugh.

Wally listened—but he never laughed.

Wally was still not happy.

Wally was not a jolly monster!

"Look at this," said Holly.

"Look at the funny face!"

The funny face made Holly laugh.

Wally looked—and looked.

What a funny face!

Wally laughed and laughed.

Wally was a jolly monster too!